WODGE
and Friends

For Henry John Duggan, with love.
Could there be a mystery in your garden? – C.A.M

For Emily. – *S.C*

Wodge and Friends: The Mystery in the Garden
published in 2021 by
Hardie Grant Children's Publishing
Wurundjeri Country
Ground Floor, Building 1, 658 Church Street
Richmond, Victoria 3121, Australia
www.hardiegrantchildrenspublishing.com

Series design by Julia Donkersley
Illustrations by Sam Caldwell

A catalogue record for this
book is available from the
National Library of Australia

Hardie Grant acknowledges the Traditional Owners of the country on which we
work, the Wurundjeri people of the Kulin nation and the Gadigal people of the Eora
nation, and recognises their continuing connection to the land, waters and culture.
We pay our respects to their Elders past, present and emerging.

Printed in Australia by Griffin Press, part of Ovato, an Accredited
ISO AS/NZS 14001 Environmental Management System printer.

1 3 5 7 9 10 8 6 4 2

WODGE
and Friends

The Mystery in the Garden

BY CAROL ANN MARTIN
ART BY SAM CALDWELL

Hardie Grant
CHILDREN'S PUBLISHING

CHAPTER ONE

'I'm not going!'

That was my little brother. His name is Dom, short for Dominic. He's seven and a bit and when he yells he means it.

'Yes, you are going!' I said. I'm Nancy and I'm nearly eleven. Our mum died when Dom was a baby and sometimes I have to be in charge. Like now.

Dad sat at the table in his pyjamas, stirring marmalade into his coffee and reading a book about

Antarctica. He didn't seem to have heard Dom.

'I am not going to stay with Miss Heavy Belly!' Dom smacked his spoon into his cornflakes and milk splattered across the table. Dad wiped his glasses and carried on reading.

'Her name is Miss Heatherbell,' I told Dom sternly. 'And we have to stay with her.'

I didn't know if I wanted to go and stay with a strange woman either. But I know there was no use yelling about it.

Dad is a photographer. His name is Harry Hamlyn and he's quite well-known. He had been asked to go to Antarctica to take photos for a book about an elephant seal named Brian. He was getting ready to go, but he had almost forgotten one thing. Where were Dom and I going to stay while he was away?

We couldn't stay with Gran. She was living in a tree so that the council couldn't chop it down and looking after four orphaned baby possums at the same time. We could stay with Auntie Pam in Darwin. But Auntie Pam was so bossy, and we'd have to go to a different school and everything. We didn't want that.

Then, that morning, Gran had rung up from her tree. 'The children can stay with my friend Miss Heatherbell,' Gran had told Dad. 'She is quite an unusual artist and she would love to have them.'

That was when Dom started yelling. Today he was Batman and his eyes glared through the slits in his mask. 'I don't care what her name is. I'm going to the South Pole with Dad.'

At last Dad looked up from his book. 'It gets a bit cold there, Dom,' he said. 'This afternoon we'll go and meet Miss Heatherbell. I'll pick you up after school.'

4

Dom stopped yelling and just sulked instead. But that was OK. I wanted to finish my breakfast and my Awesome Girl story. I have a lot of these stories about a grade-four kid who turns into a superhero, but nobody knows it's her. I make her adventures up in my head. One day I'll write them down.

Dom was still sulking as we walked to the school bus. 'I bet Miss Hefty Bull is really weird,' he grumbled.

'It's "Heatherbell",' I said. 'And if she's a friend of Gran, of course she'll be weird.'

Then Dom had a thought that cheered him up. 'Dad will probably forget to pick us up this afternoon anyway.'

I sighed because he was probably right, and everything would be left to me to get sorted.

CHAPTER TWO

As soon as we got to school, Dom took off to find his friend Sammi. I was looking around for my mate Arlo when I heard voices across the playground chanting *dummy, dummy, dumb-bum!*

I knew what that was about: Stewie MacGubbin. Stewie was a bully. He didn't go around bashing people or giving them horsebites or anything like that. He was too smart to get himself into trouble.

Stewie was good at the sly, nasty stuff that got *other* kids into trouble. He also liked teasing and calling names. And he especially liked getting a gang of kids to pick on just one kid – usually a younger kid. Today that kid was Dom.

There's nothing wrong with Dom's name. It's like a drumbeat. But Stewie and his mates liked to call him Dumb-bum. Dom could handle that, because he knew he was smarter than they were. Sammi was good at ignoring Stewie's gang, too. She stuck her arm around Dom's shoulder, her nose in the air, and the pair of them stalked off. But Arlo went tearing over and started yelling at Stewie's gang. 'Shut up, why don't you! Nobody's as dumb as you lot!'

Mr Bunsen was on playground duty and he marched up and started blaming Arlo! Stewie and his mates went off sniggering while Mr Bunsen barked at Arlo to stop being so noisy and rude.

Anyway, that was Stewie, and the best thing was to take no notice of him. But he hadn't finished yet. Part of Stewie's nastiness was that he was into payback.

Our first lesson was English and when we went to get our books out, Arlo's were sopping wet; every single book in his bag, all his homework and, worst of all, two school library books. The lid of his drink bottle was loose and water had leaked everywhere. That got him another telling off and a note to tell his mother she'd have to pay for the library books. Arlo was hot in the face and the closest I'd seen him to crying since we'd all cried on our first day at kinder.

'That lid was on tight,' he growled. 'I know it was.'

I believed him. We only had to look at Stewie's gloating face to know who'd sneaked into Arlo's bag. It had been a good day for Stewie: picking on Dom and getting Arlo into trouble twice. He didn't try anything else, but we were watching him.

At lunchtime I sat under a tree with Arlo and told him the latest thing that had happened to me. He knew my dad was a bit different to some dads and he knew my gran lived in a tree, so he hadn't been all that surprised to hear about the South Pole and Brian the elephant seal. Now I told him that Dom and I had to go and check out a whacky friend of Gran's to see if we wanted to stay with her.

'It's her or Auntie Pam,' I said.

'Hmm,' he said. 'I reckon I'd go for Miss Heatherbell.'

Just then Dom came trailing over with Sammi. He was wearing his Batman mask, but he didn't look happy.

'I don't like my lunch, Nancy,' he complained. 'Tuna and honey don't go.' In our house we all packed our own lunches.

'Too bad,' I said. 'I've eaten all of mine.'

'Don't worry about him,' Sammi told me. 'I've given him one of my kebabs, so he can't be that hungry.'

'And Miss Heatherbell will probably give us some afternoon tea,' I reminded him.

Dom stuck out his bottom lip. 'I'm not going to Miss Featherjelly's!' he roared. Then he stomped

11

off and I gave another sigh.

'Ah well, he was hoping this morning that Dad would forget to pick us up, and that could easily happen.'

'I reckon,' said Arlo.

'Maybe you could both stay with us,' offered Sammi kindly. 'Only our house is a bit small.'

But … surprise! Dad was outside the school gates at three o'clock. He was still wearing his pyjama trousers and he had on one red sock and one yellow one. But he had remembered.

CHAPTER THREE

There was at least one good thing about Miss Heatherbell. She lived much nearer to our school and our friends than we did.

When we pulled up in the car, we looked out at a tall hedge clipped to look like a row of snails with teapots on their backs instead of shells. There was a really ordinary-looking house on the right. On the left of the snail hedge, a narrow laneway ran down between Miss Heatherbell's wooden side fence and the brick wall of another ordinary-looking house.

13

We wondered what the neighbours thought about the very unusual hedge.

We got out onto the footpath and peered over a fancy iron gate set in an archway in the hedge.

'This is it,' said Dad hopefully, and for once he'd got it right.

Miss Heatherbell's house was anything but ordinary. There was a paved pathway from the gate to the veranda, but otherwise the house looked as though it was standing with its feet in a wildflower meadow. Poppies, daisies, cornflowers, sunflowers and lupins grew knee-high among grasses that wouldn't have known what a mower looked like.

The house itself was big and old. It had a wide veranda with carved wooden posts, a tall front door and a lot of large windows, all with panels of coloured flower-patterned glass.

There was a little tower on the roof that looked quite mysterious. What a great place for writing stories!

Already Dom was forgetting to sulk. 'I should have been Merlin the Magician today,' he said.

The front door opened and Miss Heatherbell came whizzing down a ramp onto the front path. Nobody had told us that she was in a wheelchair. She went faster than I could go on my skateboard! Her rainbow hair and orange scarf flew and her earrings jangled. About twenty guinea pigs came scampering after her, making excited little honking squeaks.

Up on the veranda, a big cushiony woman with a huge smile stood and waved. We soon found out that was Mrs Pikelet. She helped look after Miss Heatherbell and the house.

It seemed as though Miss Heatherbell really wanted us to stay with her. 'You are just the kind of children this house longs for,' she said. 'We especially like Batman. But you two must decide if you like the house.'

She asked Mrs Pikelet to make some afternoon tea, and she and Dad sat on the veranda to talk. 'Nancy, Dom, you go and explore,' she said. 'Go wherever you please.' So we did.

I remembered that Gran had said Miss Heatherbell was an unusual artist. We just didn't know how unusual. The first thing we saw in the hall was a row of six pink unicorns. OK, they weren't real – they were made of painted wood. One unicorn had an umbrella hanging on its horn. Another had a big hat

17

with yellow daisies, another a purple cloak. While we were staring at these unusual clothes hooks, a giant clock on the wall flew open and a stuffed duck burst out. It quacked loudly at us four times and flew back in.

'Wow!' gasped Dom. 'That is so cool! It would be a lot easier to tell the time if all we had to do was count the quacks.'

It was a strange house with lots of passageways and lots of doors. We opened one door and found ourselves under the sea. Well, it was really the bathroom, but the walls and ceiling were painted in swirls of blue and green. Coloured fish swam around rolling big googly eyes, and an octopus peeked out from the waving weeds. The bath was a rock pool and there was a mermaid sitting in it. Even the toilet was shaped like a rock. But Dom sat on it and it was nice and bouncy.

Another door led into Miss Heatherbell's studio.

18

Her paintings were everywhere. Some leaned in rows against the walls and some were propped up on easels. Mostly they were pictures of blue, orange and green guinea pigs peeping out of coloured splodges.

A little further down the main passageway, we heard a lovely sound. It was mellow and musical, like ancient bells from some mystical place.

The sound was coming from behind a door painted with a froth of pink-and-white blossoms. I slowly opened the door and the music of the mysterious bells grew louder. We were looking into a large room with a floor so shiny it could have been the surface of a lake. In the centre of the floor was a low, oblong table with richly coloured cushions placed around it. Here and there were bamboo-and-paper screens painted with sprays of cherry blossom in the same pink and white as the door. The walls were snow white and instead of pictures, they were hung with Japanese fans and kimonos.

As we stood and gazed, we realised that the musical sound was coming from the open window, where strings of wooden wind chimes were gently swinging in the breeze.

It was all so peaceful and serene, but we couldn't stay – we still had more exploring to do.

This time it wasn't a sound that led us on, but a smell. The warm, sweet aroma of baking wafted up from a side passageway and enticed us along to the kitchen.

Sure enough, Mrs Pikelet was in there, busily taking fresh scones off a cooling tray and onto a serving plate. 'Hello dearies,' she beamed.

It was a cosy room. That was probably because there were fiery red dragons twisting and twirling themselves around the walls and breathing out flames.

'Lovely and warm in winter,' said Mrs Pikelet.

The kitchen table was round, like the one in King Arthur's castle. There was a big silver sword with a jewelled hilt in the middle of the table. 'Excalibur,' I whispered to Dom. 'King Arthur's magic sword.' You'd think there'd have been benches round the table, but there were wooden toadstools to sit on instead.

Dom and I knew there was lots more to see in the house, but Mrs Pikelet asked us to help her take the tea trays out onto the veranda.

I was a bit worried about Dom carrying cups, saucers and a milk jug. But he had that fierce frown that appeared on his face when he was concentrating hard, and Mrs Pikelet didn't seem at all worried. We reached the veranda safely and set out scones, jam, cream, tea and orange juice onto a table that was held up by four gingerbread men. Then we sat down.

Miss Heatherbell and Dad looked at us.

'Well?' asked Dad.

'Well?' asked Miss Heatherbell.

Dom's eyes shone through his Batman mask. 'I'm going to stay with Miss Heatherbell!' he yelled.

Phew! That was a relief, because it was exactly what I wanted, too. I knew now for sure that this house was the place where I could really start to write.

Dad looked as relieved as I was. 'Right then,' he said. He gave us a big hug each. 'Be good and I'll see you when I get back.'

'No, Dad,' I sighed. 'Today is only Monday. We haven't even packed yet. You're not going to Antarctica until Friday.'

CHAPTER FOUR

Dom and I moved into Miss Heatherbell's house on Thursday. She said we could have Friday off school to settle in. Monday was a holiday, so we had an extra-long weekend. But I don't think Miss Heatherbell would have been worried if we didn't go back to school at all. Luckily, I was still in charge – kind of.

Miss Heatherbell was so pleased to have us, and so were the guinea pigs. The guinea pigs all had names. We couldn't remember every one of them, but Miss Heatherbell could. They were very well-trained and did their little wees and poos on newspaper that was put down on the laundry floor.

Our new home was super weird, but it was a cool kind of weird. Because it was so old, there was a creakiness and creepiness about it, too. But it was a creakiness and creepiness that we liked.

And then there were our bedrooms. Unreal! It was as if Miss Heatherbell had always known who was going to come and stay with her one day. We were up in the tower, and it had once been one big room. But at some time a wooden partition had been built down the middle so that Dom and I each had our own place, but right next door to each other. Our windows were side by side and looked out onto the back garden. If we slid them up, we could lean out and talk to each other as if we were in the same room.

When I walked into my room, I was in a woodland glade – all midnight blue and moonlight silver. The walls were painted with big, shadowy trees and the carpet beneath my feet felt like grass. My ceiling was billows of deep-blue gauze scattered with stars and my bed was a scooped-out log with a soft, mossy mattress and a doona and pillow of patchwork leaves.

In one corner there was a real tree trunk and when I opened a door in the bark, I was looking into my wardrobe. The only other furniture was a desk and chair of rustic wood, and a lamp in the shape of a full moon. I laid my new blue notebook

and pencil on the desk that just seemed to have been
waiting there just for me.

But that wasn't all. I was not alone in that room.

There were faces peeping down from among the leaves. This time the faces didn't belong to guinea pigs, but to strange, skinny little sprite-ish thingies with tilted eyes and pointy noses and sly, secretive smiles. When I looked carefully, I could see glimpses of cobwebby clothes and dragonfly wings. They were odd creatures, but I was OK with them.

Dom's room was a desert island. Honestly, the floor was golden and crunchy underfoot, like walking on a beach. His walls had trees, too, but these were palms, with rainbow parrots and coconuts and whole troops of monkeys. Behind the trees a schooner was anchored in a sparkling blue bay, with a skull-and-crossbones fluttering in the wind. In one corner of his room a large X was painted on the wall and beneath it, atop a pile of sand, was a big brass-bound chest for Dom to keep his treasures in. His bed was a coracle that actually bobbed up and down. I had a go in it and it made me a bit queasy, but Dom thought it was brilliant.

On our first night in the house, we lay and listened to all the strange creaks and bumps and rattles. There was even an owl that appeared just before dark. Big and shadowy, he slowly swooped over the rooftop like something in a Halloween movie.

'Do you reckon there could be a ghost?' Dom called to me.

'Could be,' I agreed. I was already getting some ideas for a super goosebump-y story, *Awesome Girl and the Haunted House,* so I hopped out of bed and quickly wrote them down.

As well as a cool, creepy house, Miss Heatherbell had the *biggest* back garden. The house stood at one end and a high wooden fence ran around the other sides, with a wooden gate leading out into the lane. A few steps outside the back door was a cluster of bushes. But just as the front hedge was a row of snails with teapots, these bushes were all in the shape of pigs. Not only that, they were pigs with wings. They were like that saying, 'Pigs might fly'. They weren't off the ground yet, but looked as if they could be at any minute.

It was easy to walk between the almost-flying pigs and onto a huge lawn. At the top end of the lawn stood Mrs Pikelet's clothes hoist, and that was interesting. It was a silver rocket ship with its nose pointing up into the sky as if it were zooming towards outer space, trailing sheets, towels, socks, shirts, undies and whatever else Mrs Pikelet had pegged onto its tail.

At the bottom of the garden was a tumbledown shed and an old, empty greenhouse with dirty, broken panes. That was a wild and forgotten place; it looked like nobody had been there in years. The rest of the garden was just lawn and guinea pigs. Or so we thought.

On our first Saturday morning, we took our

cricket set out for a game on the back lawn. I let Dom bat first because it was easy to get him out. But this time he was wearing his magic gumboots. I don't know if they helped, but he swiped at the ball, knocked it for six and nearly fell over. Then he yelled, dropped the bat and put his hands over his ears. That was because the ball was heading straight for the old greenhouse. We waited for the crash of breaking glass. But it never came. The ball rocketed over the greenhouse and landed … where?

We went to take a closer look. The space between the shed and the greenhouse was very narrow. It was filled with a tangle of long grass, weeds, straggly bushes and blackberry brambles. *No way are you coming through here*, they seemed to say.

Saying "no way" to Dom and me is the best way to make us find a way. We knelt down and started looking.

Then a guinea pig went scuttling past us and

straight through the tangle of greenery. It might have been Freddy, or maybe Lulu.

'Well, if he can, we can,' said Dom.

CHAPTER FIVE

We peered and poked at the spot where Freddy, or Lulu, had gone through. Sure enough, there was a space where there was more grass than tangle. It was only a small space, and the grass was tall and thick and didn't want to let us through. But after pushing, squeezing and wriggling for what seemed like a long time, my head finally burst out into a kind of clearing behind the shed and the greenhouse. I forced the rest of myself through and then helped

Dom to crawl in after me. We were both scratched and prickled all over our arms, and Dom's T-shirt was ripped. But we stood up and looked around. There was still a lot of grass and weeds, and the back fence that closed us in was held up by creepers. It surely was a secret, hidden place – it had that grassy, earthy, old and forgotten sort of smell.

'So, you're in, are you?' snapped a narky voice. 'I suppose you're the nincompoops who whacked that ball over. Well, thank you very much! You nearly knocked my head off!'

Dom grabbed my arm and stared. I stared where he was staring. Through the long grass, something stared back.

It could have been a giant toad. It had big, bulging eyes, a flat nose and a wide, floppy mouth like a toad. It was warty and lumpy like a toad. It squatted like a toad. But it also had vampire teeth, clawed feet, pointy ears and a pair of bat wings.

'Is that what said something just now?' asked Dom.

'It's a statue,' I said. 'Statues don't talk.' I put myself between my little brother and the monster thingy. 'Don't be scared.'

'I'm not,' said Dom and pushed himself back in front to have a good squiz.

We could both see now that the beast was made of stone. It was even covered in green and red mossy stuff from being there for ages. More of Miss Heatherbell's work? I didn't think so. It was much older, and Miss Heatherbell couldn't have got her wheelchair into this place anyway.

We stood and watched as, all by itself, the statue slowly fell over backwards. Where it had crouched, there was a hole in the ground.

A voice came out of the hole. It wasn't the cranky voice we'd heard before. This one was deep and gurgly. 'Hast they gonded?'

When a deep voice comes up out of the ground, it's a good idea to hide. I pulled Dom back into the bushes and we crouched down. But we just had to keep on peering from our hiding place. Something was going to come out of that hole, and we didn't know what. I held tightly to Dom's hand, ready to push, drag and bundle him out of this place if I had to.

41

The first thing to creep up was a head. It was covered in thick, tangled curls about the same colour as toffee. Two huge, dark eyes peered around, and a long, leathery sort of snout snuffled at the air as though it was trying to sniff me and Dom out. We crouched down lower and tried not to breathe.

Whatever it was, it must have felt safe. With a lot of rumbling and grunting, it reached out its monkey-like paws and hauled its round body out of the hole. Then it stood up and shook the soil out of its curls. It was about the size of a wombat, but stood up on its back legs, and slowly blinked.

'Ooh!' whispered Dom. 'What is it, Nancy?'

He shouldn't have done that. The thing rolled its eyes in our direction, gave a rumbling cry and tumbled headfirst straight back into its hole.

CHAPTER SIX

I just sat and gaped and wondered what we'd been looking at. But Dom went running over to the hole. 'It might have hurt itself!' he cried.

I ran after him and we both looked down into the hole. It wasn't a very deep hole, and it had a bed of dried grass and leaves. The thing was right way up and gazing back at us. It didn't seem to be hurt, but *eeww, pooh!!*

Dom and I reeled back, covering our noses. Never

in my life had I smelled anything like the stink that came from that creature. Rotten fish, dead rats, filthy socks, dog poo and a blocked drain, and that was just for a start. It was gross. Worse than gross. As we gagged and flapped at the air, the thing tried to pull the statue back over its hole.

'Nay! Nay!' it shouted. 'Wodge doth want not to! Wodge wishn't! Wodge willn't!' It reminded me of the tantrums Dom used to throw when he was two, except that it used even weirder words than Dom did. And at two, Dom used some weird words!

I pinched my nose hard and trod on the statue so that it couldn't drop down.

'You don't want to do what?' I asked.

The voice that answered came from behind me. 'He doesn't want to be famous, bubble brain. He doesn't want to be on the telly.'

I spun around and accidentally lifted my foot. The statue swung back into the hole like a plug in a bathtub, with only a few airholes under the claws of the stone beast.

'Ah!' Dom was disappointed. He shoved at the statue, but it wouldn't budge.

'Never mind,' I said. I was already pushing my way through the grass and weeds. 'There's somebody else in here.'

The first voice we'd heard had spoken again, scratchy and cross. I followed the sound as it nattered away.

'You come walloping in here like a pair of elephants. You uptilt the gargoyle and frighten Wodge. Who do you think you are? Eh? Eh?'

The smell, thank goodness, was fading. I could also see that Dom was getting cranky himself.

'It's just a parrot,' he said to me. 'Or a cocky. It's really grumpy, whatever it is.'

47

What we found in the grass was a fairy. Well, it was another statue, just like the toady vampire thingy, but definitely a fairy. She had a frilly frock, flowers in her hair and butterfly wings. This one was also stained green and red from being there for a long time.

'Is this it, then?' asked Dom. 'A statue that talks?'

''Course I can flippin' well talk!' snapped the stone fairy. 'It's all I *can* do. Stuck here, year in, year out. Can't move, can't go anywhere. Stuck! Stuck!

48

Stuck!' She sounded as though she was blaming us.

'It's not our fault you can't move. Statues aren't supposed to move,' I told her.

'This one's mouth moves,' said Dom.

'It's the only bit of me that does,' grumbled the fairy. Then she was off again. 'Who said it was your fault? It was that fiddler's fault, Felix Frizzwort. Scrape, scrape, scrape, squawk and squeak on his fiddle all night long to the moon. As if the moon would want to listen to a racket like that. So I threw a statue spell at him.' She was getting screechier by the second. 'The spell bounced off his fiddle stick, didn't it? Bounced right back and hit me, didn't it?'

I knew Dom was trying not to laugh.

'Why don't you just undo the spell?' he asked.

'How can I, you dippy goose?' screamed the statue. 'I'd have to wave my arms about to do that!'

I could tell she wasn't thrilled to see us, but after all the trouble we'd taken to get in there, I thought we should at least get to know each other.

'I'm Nancy Hamlyn,' I politely told her. 'And this is my brother, Dom.'

'Never heard of you,' she said crabbily. 'And I'm not going to tell you who I am, because it's none of your business.'

Well, we didn't need her name – to me she was already the BTF: Bad-Tempered Fairy.

'Can't you do any magic at all, then?' I asked, just to change the subject.

'I can do a bit,' the BTF replied. 'But you try casting spells when the only thing that moves is your mouth.'

Just when she was about as loud as she could get, she stopped. Her lips turned to stone and she was as silent as … well, as a statue. I wondered if she ran on batteries and needed a recharge.

'Psst!' Dom gave me a nudge. I followed his eyes and groaned.

CHAPTER SEVEN

Next door, close to the fence, there was an old pear tree. It didn't have any pears, but it looked great for climbing. Someone was climbing it now. As we watched, a red, sweaty face appeared above the fence. But it wasn't just any red, sweaty face.

'It's Stewie MacGubbin,' groaned Dom.

And that was when we found out that Stewie lived right next door to Miss Heatherbell. It wasn't a trick of the mind. It wasn't a bad dream. There he was, staring at us from the pear tree.

'Who's there with you?' he asked. His eyes gleamed with curiosity. 'Who's that I heard screeching just now?'

He couldn't see the BTF hidden in the grass, and I wasn't going to tell him.

'It was me,' I said quickly. 'Just me.'

Stewie's mean look got meaner. 'It didn't sound like you.'

I gave a blood-freezing scream. 'Bull ants! I got bitten by a bull ant!' Then I hopped about a bit. 'Ouch! Ouch! Ouchie!'

But Stewie's blood didn't freeze. He just looked at me with a sneer. 'Nah, there's somebody else there.'

I wanted Stewie to go away. Weird things were happening for sure. But they were our weird things, not his.

Then, like magic, our rescue came.

'Stooooweee!' a voice called from the MacGubbins' back door. 'Stooooweee, you get down from that tree and you come inside. Now!!'

There was one person Stewie didn't argue with. That person was his mum. He slithered down through the branches and we heard him running to the house.

'That was lucky,' I said.

'Luck?' The BTF's mouth seemed to be working again. 'That wasn't luck, that was me.'

Mrs MacGubbin's voice came again. This time, it was right behind us. 'On Saturdays, I – Mrs MacGubbin – have my bagpipe lesson. I make Stewie go out to play. I only called him in again so he'd leave you lot alone.'

Dom and I gaped at the space where there was a voice, but no Mrs MacGubbin. The BTF cackled fiendishly.

'It *was* you,' I said. 'You're a ventriloquist.'

The BTF got even cacklier. 'Just as well I am. I don't want him buzzing around.' Then she said in her usual crabby way, 'And you two can scram as well. Nobody asked you to come here. Poor Wodge, he'll be so upset.'

I guessed that Wodge was the creature hiding under the gargoyle. 'Why is he so shy?' I asked.

'What's he scared of?'

The BTF explained very slowly, as if we were especially stupid. 'He's the only wodge left in the world, right? They used to be everywhere. Just like the dinosaurs, only smaller, OK? But like the dinosaurs, they died out. Not surprising when all the wodges had to defend themselves with was a pong. If people catch him now, they'll put him in a zoo or a museum or something. They'll put him on television. They'll take photos of him with their phones and pose for selfies with him. They'll post him on the internet. He doesn't want that!'

OK, but there was something I had to ask. 'If he's so shy and you can't move, how did the two of you find out about all those things that have got him so worried?'

'The guinea pigs,' said the BTF. 'They tell us. They sit on Miss Heatherbell's lap when she's on her computer. They watch her TV. And they don't just poop on those newspapers, you know. They actually read them!'

Then Dom said, 'What if we don't tell anyone we found Wodge? Could we be secret friends with him?'

'It would be a secret,' I promised. 'If he'd just come out again.'

The BTF didn't say a word. She was just an old garden ornament again. Was all this real, or were we imagining it? Could Dom and I imagine exactly the same things at the same time? It was all getting a bit freaky.

CHAPTER EIGHT

As well as freaky, it was also starting to feel like lunchtime. Miss Heatherbell didn't always remember about meals. But if she did, she might start to wheel herself around looking for us. Best to be somewhere she could find us.

The BTF was still playing statues. But how could we be sure?

'It's been very nice to meet you,' said Dom.

'We'll come back,' I said.

Silence.

All right, if that was how she was going to be.

We crawled our way back through to the lawn, where one of the fatter guinea pigs was waiting for us. As we stood up, it spoke to us with the voice of the BTF.

We could see the pigs-might-fly bushes and the roof with our little tower. We could see our cricket stumps still stuck in the lawn. It all looked so normal. But the weird things that had just happened to us really *had* happened. It was exciting and flabbergasting at the same time. One thing we knew for sure: Wodge and the BTF had to be a secret.

We went in the back door and along a passageway that Miss Heatherbell had turned into a magic forest. Glittery wolves grinned at us and bears blew bubbles at us until we came to the dragon kitchen. There was no sign of lunch, but Mrs Pikelet had left a note: *Gone to yoga. Quiche in fridge. See you later xxx.* Good old Mrs P!

There was no sign of Miss Heatherbell, and obviously no rush to have lunch after all. Dom picked up Excalibur and began waving it at the dragons on the wall, with lots of leaping and prancing and shouting of *'en garde!'* and *'touché!'* I left him to it and went up to my room to do something important.

My notebook was on my desk, where I'd started Chapter One of *Awesome Girl and the Haunted House*. But now I had to urgently scribble down everything I could remember about that morning and what we'd discovered in the wild place at the bottom of the garden. When I was sure I'd thought of everything, I put my notebook and pencil into the back pocket of my jeans. From now on, I'd be taking notes every chance I got.

Then I went down and collected Dom, who was still fighting dragons in the kitchen. It was high time we reminded Miss Heatherbell about lunch.

We found her doing wheelies around the hall, trying to round up guinea pigs.

'Horrie!' she cried. 'Come here this minute!'

Dom did his famous magical gumboot leap. He grabbed a scampering bundle of fur and put it in her lap. Luckily it was Horrie.

'Thank you, Dom,' Miss Heatherbell beamed.

'Mrs Pikelet has left us a quiche,' I told her.

'Lovely!' she said. 'I'll just put these rascals down for their nap and we'll all have lunch.'

Dom and I were on our way back to the kitchen when the front doorbell rang. We stopped and watched Miss Heatherbell roll to the door and open it.

Oh no! There stood Stewie MacGubbin. He must have found out that it wasn't his mum who had called him. Now he'd come stickybeaking to see what was going on.

I grabbed Dom and we crouched behind a polka-dotted warthog umbrella stand to do some stickybeaking of our own.

Stewie smiled at Miss Heatherbell. It was like being smiled at by a shark.

'Good afternoon, Miss Heatherbell.'

What a nice, polite boy. Yuck. I started to feel sick.

65

'I hope you don't mind me coming around,' Stewie went on. 'But there's something I have to tell you. That boy, I think his name's Dumbo something, him and his sister have been right down at the bottom of your yard.'

Now I felt not just sick, but doomed as well. Stewie knew something and he was about to dob. Dom screwed up his face and we waited for our secret to be blabbed.

'They were talking and poking around and I heard some other voices, strange voices. One was

66

really shouty.' Stewie gave her the shark smile again. 'I thought you'd want to know. They're up to some funny things down there.'

Miss Heatherbell smiled back at Stewie. 'The world is full of funny things, dear,' she said. Then she closed the door. 'I don't think we like him much, do we, darlings?' she sighed.

We weren't sure if she was talking to us or to the guinea pigs.

Well, like him or not (mostly not), one thing was for sure: Stewie MacGubbin had his spotty nose on our scent and, knowing him, he wasn't going to stop sniffing. That could make things quite tricky.

CHAPTER NINE

I was warming the quiche and setting the table for lunch when Dom came back into the kitchen. He was wearing his detective hat and he peered at me through a magnifying glass.

'Nancy, do you think there's really only one wodge left in the world?' he asked me. 'People know about dinosaurs and hairy mammoths and things like that. I think we should try to find out if anybody knows about wodges.'

'OK,' I said. 'But don't tell them there's one at the bottom of our garden, OK?'

I took out my notebook and, turning to a clean page, I began to draw. By the time Miss Heatherbell rolled into the kitchen, I had finished a drawing of Wodge.

We showed it to Miss Heatherbell. 'Do you know what this is?' Dom asked her in a stern detective voice.

Miss Heatherbell looked at the drawing for a long time. Then she said, 'Oh!' in a puzzled kind of way. She put on her spectacles and looked again. 'No, I don't know what it is, dears. Except, perhaps … maybe a long time ago … a dream?' Her voice faded away and she shook her head, as if she were trying to clear a mist. We waited. 'No, I couldn't tell you,' she said at last.

So that was that. We had quiche and salad and Miss Heatherbell said she hoped we weren't bored living with her.

'I do get quite lost in my painting,' she said. 'Sometimes I even forget what day it is.'

We promised her we weren't bored.

Down in the hall, the doorbell rang. What if it was Stewie again? I raced to answer it before he could do any more snitching. But it was Arlo. I'd forgotten he was coming around that afternoon.

Seeing Arlo gave me an idea. He knew a lot

about Australian animals and the ancient history of Australia. Maybe he knew about wodges way back in time. All three of us went up to my room and I showed Arlo my Wodge drawing. Like Miss Heatherbell, he looked at it for a long time.

'Nope,' he said at last. 'Never seen anything like that. But we'd better ask Mum and Dad.'

Arlo's family had a gallery filled with awesome Aboriginal art. They sold paintings and books, jewellery made from shells and some cool woven baskets. They knew even more than Arlo did about this country's animals, so we went to ask them.

But neither Arlo's mum nor his dad had ever seen anything quite like Wodge. We looked at the huge, brilliantly coloured and patterned paintings hung on the gallery walls. We saw kangaroos, koalas, eagles and emus, crocodiles and snakes and all kinds of creatures. But there was no sign of Wodge.

Arlo had another idea. 'We could ask Sammi.

They might have had wodges where she came from.'

Sammi, short for Samira, had come to Australia with her mum and two younger sisters because there was a war in their country.

Sammi lived down the street from the gallery. You just followed the scent of honey, spices and vanilla to their tiny house. That was because Sammi's mum, Mrs Yusef, baked cakes for the Whole World Café. But this afternoon the family was out in the backyard. Sammi was playing with her little sisters, while her mum was doing her English homework. Mrs Yusef was always busy, yet she still found time to study.

They were all pleased to see us. Mrs Yusef raced away to get cold drinks and homemade biscuits. When she came back, we showed my drawing to her and Sammi. We could tell by Mrs Yusef's face that she'd never seen a wodge before. 'This is

73

Australian?' she asked.

Sammi explained that we were asking if they had ever heard of wodges in their country. That made her mum laugh.'We have legends about genies,' Sammi told us.

'Like in *Aladdin*?' asked Arlo.

'Sort of,' said Sammi. 'The genies can turn themselves into anything they want. But I don't think they'd want to look like a wodge, do you?'

74

Then Arlo said, 'What's this all about, anyway, Nancy? Don't tell me you've seen one of these wodgie thingos.'

Dom and I looked at each other. This wasn't good. We wanted to tell him. We wanted to tell Sammi, too. Keeping stuff from your best friends sucks!

CHAPTER TEN

When the two of us were on our way home, Dom said, 'Do you think Wodge would let Sammi and Arlo be his secret friends as well?'

I didn't know. I didn't even know if Wodge would let me and Dom be his friends. Maybe we'd never see him again.

It was nearly teatime, but Miss Heatherbell was still in her studio. Dom and I walked very quietly past. But Miss Heatherbell called out, 'Come in!' as though we had knocked. So in we went. Miss Heatherbell was sitting in her wheelchair in front of a painting that was propped on an easel.

'I've just finished it,' she told us happily. 'What do you think?'

We had no idea what the painting was supposed to be of, but it was totally cool to look at. Kind of like it had rained parrot poop and custard in the Botanical Gardens. The trick was to find the guinea pigs. There were always guinea pigs in Miss Heatherbell's paintings. Dom went up close with his magnifying glass and made *aha!* detective noises. I looked and looked and at last I saw a little furry face peering out of a green splodge. But it wasn't a guinea pig.

'That's Wodge!' I cried.

'It is!' Dom was as amazed as I was. 'It's *him*.'

Miss Heatherbell put on her spectacles and peered. 'That's a guinea pig, dears,' she said. 'It's not a very good one and I shall do it again. But it is meant to be a guinea pig.'

77

Miss Heatherbell was not the kind of person to tell lies. She really believed she'd painted a guinea pig, so we didn't argue with her.

'But it is Wodge,' Dom whispered to me as we went down to the kitchen.

Miss Heatherbell was quite hungry after all of her painting. So the three of us helped Mrs Pikelet make heaps of scrambled eggs and toast, with bananas and ice-cream for afters.

I wondered if Dom and I should go back to the secret place before bedtime, although I wasn't sure. Perhaps we'd find absolutely nothing there but weeds, bushes and brambles. But after we'd helped Mrs Pikelet wash up, Miss Heatherbell was keen for us to play a game she'd made up called The Sword and the Spectre.

To do this, we went into the Snug. After my own room and the kitchen, this was my favourite place in the house. Just like its name, the Snug was a cosy little sitting room that could have been in a country cottage, except that Miss Heatherbell had created yet another enchanted place. It was for all the world as though we were down beneath the roots of a huge, very old tree.

The roots, all gnarled and twisted, formed the ceiling and framed the window. The floor was earthy brown with rag rugs like red-and-yellow autumn leaves. The chairs were the sink-in kind and patterned with wildflowers like the front garden was. There was even an old-fashioned fireplace with a mantelpiece, but because it was summer, a pot of flowers stood in the hearth.

That room made me think of long-ago picture books, maybe even ones that my mother read to me. I can't remember them clearly, but I almost expected to see rabbits in waistcoats or pinafores hopping around in that little burrow.

The Sword and the Spectre was a great game. We'd take it in turns to spin Excalibur on the table and whoever the sword pointed to when it came to rest had to tell a ghost story. Mrs Pikelet had first go and she told us about *The Ghost in the Fridge*. Dom's story was *Spiderman and the Phantom Underpants*, Miss Heatherbell's was called *The Headless Horseman Wins Again*, and I told my story, *Awesome Girl and the Mystery of the Ghastly Eyeballs in the Night*. I'd already started writing down my ideas for this and it was good to try it out on an audience. It was fun, but the two of us still had other mysterious things to think about, and things that I needed to write down. Later on, before we got into bed, Dom and I learnt out of our side-by-side open windows and talked to each other.

'Nancy,' said Dom. 'How did Wodge get into Miss Heatherbell's painting?'

'She put him there,' I said. 'But the weird thing is,

I'm sure she doesn't know she did.'

It was nearly dark and we were both in bed when Dom called to me again. 'Nancy, the owl's back!'

Ah, the ghostly owl! I climbed out of my log and we both went back to lean out of our windows and watch it swoop and glide, a majestic figure against the evening sky. But this time was a bit different.

83

Something like a firecracker whooshed up from behind the greenhouse. A beam of pink light hit the owl in mid-soar. It gave an un-majestic squawk and tumbled into a double somersault. When it flipped itself right side up again, it was a brilliant pink and was even more starry-eyed than an owl is supposed to be. With another squawk, it flapped its ruffled wings, turned around and headed for home.

It was followed by a high-pitched cackle that we both knew well.

'The BTF,' I said. 'Doing a bit of magic.'

'Just showing off,' said Dom.

CHAPTER ELEVEN

On Sunday mornings, Miss Heatherbell liked to sleep in and Mrs Pikelet went to church. Dom and I had heaps of time to go down to the secret place before breakfast. We wanted to talk to Wodge so much. Even to see Wodge would do.

'Bring ice-cream.' That was what the BTF had said through the guinea pig.

I got a bowl from the cupboard and we scooped some neapolitan ice-cream into it. We weren't sure if it was for Wodge or the BTF. But we'd been told to bring it, and we were bringing it.

Our plan was to sneak into the secret place without anyone knowing we were coming. But crawling through tangled bushes with a bowl of ice-cream isn't easy and it isn't quiet.

At first we thought we were in luck. As my head came through into the grassy patch, I saw that the gargoyle was flat on its back behind the open hole. Wodge was lying in the sun and seemed to be asleep. But not for long.

'Uh-oh, here comes trouble!' muttered a voice we knew. The BTF was lurking where she always lurked. No hope of sneaking up on her.

Wodge opened his eyes and tottered to his feet.

'Don't go, Wodge!' I cried. 'We brought ice-cream!'

'And don't do the smell thing!' cried Dom.

We scrambled out of the bushes, but too late.

Wodge let out a burbled yell. 'Alack, forsooth and great lizard's gizzards!'

I couldn't always understand the words, but his meaning was clear. Wodge was soon in his hole and pulling down the gargoyle. At least he didn't make the smell, and we could see his eyes peering through the claw holes.

The BTF, friendly as ever, called out, 'Buzz off, you two. It was peaceful here until you came back.' At least her words were easy to understand.

I knew Wodge was watching us, and I wondered

if I could bluff him into coming out.

'We'd better go, but at least we tried,' I sighed to Dom, taking his hand as though I meant it. But the gargoyle stayed firmly down and the BTF kept up a stony silence. That left me looking a bit silly unless I really did intend for us to leave.

Dom wasn't about to give up that easily. He pulled his hand away and glared at the BTF. 'If Wodge is such a great big secret, how come Miss Heatherbell's put him in one of her paintings?' he asked.

The BTF made a dark, grumbly noise. 'It always was a leaky spell, that one.'

'What spell?' asked Dom.

'Oh, bogglification!' growled the BTF. 'The forgetting spell.'

'Tell us about it,' I said. I didn't dare whip out my notebook in case she thought I was spying, but I listened hard so that I could make notes later.

'All right.' The BTF gave up. 'Years and years ago Miss Heatherbell came down here and found us, just like you did. Her name is Clara and she was the same age as you at the time. She was as lively as you are. There wasn't all this TV and internet stuff around in those days. But they did have cameras and newspapers and museums. Wodge still had to be a secret.'

I thought about Miss Heatherbell, with a name like Clara, nine years old and not in a wheelchair.

'She would have kept the secret,' I said. It was

89

something I felt sure of.

'Perhaps she would,' the BTF agreed. 'She and Wodge were best friends.'

Dom interrupted. 'But when we showed her a drawing of Wodge, she said she didn't know anything about him.'

'It's true, she doesn't know,' the BTF said. Now, as well as sounding cranky, she sounded a bit tearful. We were amazed. It seemed the BTF did have feelings after all, at least for Miss Heatherbell. I made a note in my head to write down that sometimes bad-tempered people might just be sad.

'She doesn't know because she's forgotten,' the BTF went on. 'After one summer here with Wodge and me, Clara was sent off to boarding school.' The BTF gave a big, snuffly sniff. 'I got worried she might tell. So the day she came to say goodbye, I put the forgetting spell on her.'

'You could do that?' I asked. 'You're rubbish at

magic, but you could make Miss Heatherbell forget about Wodge and you?'

'She didn't forget just like *that*,' said the BTF. 'I made us seem fuzzy for a while, like a dream. Then we just faded away.'

This was making me and Dom sad, too. But I had a question.

'You didn't want us here, did you? So how come you didn't put the forgetting spell on us?'

'Because I've forgotten it!' howled the BTF.

That was lucky for us. I didn't want Wodge to seem like a dream. He must have decided that he didn't want to be a dream either. The next moment we heard, 'Ice-cream? Erm … ice-cream?'

The gargoyle had lifted a crack and two large, dark eyes peered out.

I waved the bowl. 'It was ice-cream, but it's gone a bit runny now.'

The gargoyle tipped back further. Wodge's head appeared. 'Runny is most slurpful,' he said.

Dom peeked into the bowl. 'It's part runny and part lumpy,' he said.

'Ooh,' gurgled Wodge. 'Wodge doth most love runny and lumpy.'

Gently, gently, fingers crossed, things were starting to look hopeful.

The BTF was running out of patience. 'For goodness sake, stop all this ditherpating and just give him the ice-cream!'

Well, she was certainly back to her grouchy self!

CHAPTER TWELVE

And that was how we became friends with Wodge. It was as easy as a bowl of ice-cream. He scrambled out of his hole and grabbed it with both paws. He might well have been mega thousands of years old, but in all that time he'd never learnt any manners. He shoved the ice-cream into his mouth, sloshing and slurping and making sucking noises like bathwater going down the plug hole. When he'd finished, he gave a deep, rumbling burp. Then he smiled.

'Hast moresome?'

'We might have,' I said. 'But first we do some talking.'

I was going to tell him about Arlo and Sammi and how good they were at keeping secrets. But that didn't happen because something else did.

'What are you doing?' asked a voice that would spread a secret from here to Darwin in five minutes.

Stewie was back.

This time he must have been standing on a stepladder. His head and shoulders were above the top of the fence and he had a *gotcha* smirk on his face.

95

The BTF, as always, was hidden in the grass. Wodge rolled silently into his hole.

'Looking for our ball,' I said, whacking at a clump of weeds.

Stewie's smirk got nastier. 'Oh yeah? Well why don't I come and help you?' he said.

I tried to think of a reason why he shouldn't climb over the fence. But while I was thinking, a reason came along all by itself. It was dark and hairy and it travelled along the fence with a steady up-and-down ripple.

Stewie's face went white and his eyes bulged. He didn't seem to be able to move. At first I thought the BTF had managed to cast another statue spell. But then Stewie gave a shriek and fell off his ladder. All we heard after that were his feet racing for home.

Who knew that Stewie was terrified of caterpillars?

'Nothing to do with me,' said the BTF. 'I was

trying to turn him into a teapot, but I have to stand on my head to do that.'

Wodge had bravely come out of his hole. 'Fie! If yon snoopsnot had over-topped the fence, Wodge would have mightily stinked him!'

I was glad it hadn't come to that.

'Look,' I said. 'Miss Heatherbell will be getting up soon and we'll be having breakfast. But we will come back.'

'With ice-cream?' asked Wodge.

I sighed. Wodge was obviously an ice-cream guts who wanted to turn me and Dom into ice-cream thieves.

'Don't you ever think about anything else?' I asked him. 'What did you do before ice-cream was invented?'

I could see that we were onto his favourite subject.

'Wodge remembers not when wast not ice-cream,' he said. 'But one thousand, two thousand and three hundred more years gone by, Wodge remembers Alexander the Great Mate. Mightiful warrior was he, mightiful king, conqueror of all ancient lands. Conquered all of Greece, conquered Turkey, conquered Persia.'

Dom was impressed. 'Wow, he did a lot of conquering!'

I could see him having an Alexander the Great day really soon.

'Can you get to the point?' screeched the BTF.

'I've heard all this a thousand times.'

Wodge chortled. 'When Alexander was not busy conquering, he loved muchly to play. Alexander and Wodge went roly-poly in the snow.'

He flopped over and rolled with his feet in the air, just to demonstrate.

'If you knew what you look like,' sniffed the BTF.

Wodge turned himself right way up and puffed. 'Alexander and Wodge, they eat the snow. But it

99

tasteth like not much exciting.'

'It tastes of nothing,' agreed Dom, who'd tried it.

'Aha!' burbled Wodge. 'Wodge hast a big idea. Alexander the Great Mate, let us put berries and honey in the snow.' He smacked his lips. 'Verily most of all things delicious.'

Ancient Greek icy poles. I could see that Wodge and his favourite food went back a long way.

'Right,' I said, getting on all fours, ready to leave. 'Back soon. Maybe there'll be ice-cream, maybe not. Depends on you, really. Are you going to be nice and not run and hide?'

CHAPTER THIRTEEN

Mrs Pikelet was home and helping Miss Heatherbell in the shower, so we got out some fruit salad and yoghurt for a late breakfast. That earned us big Pikelet hugs. While we were all at the King Arthur table, Miss Heatherbell said, 'Would you like Mrs Pikelet to put some rainbow streaks in your hair? She's going to brighten up mine today.'

'Erm … Arlo and Sammi are coming around soon,' I said.

Before Mrs Pikelet could offer to rainbow streak them, too, I quickly said, 'Thank you very much, but school won't allow it.'

'How boring of them,' said Miss Heatherbell. 'But I'm sure the four of you will find other ways to have fun.'

Dom thought he might have a Robin Hood day. Mrs Pikelet lent him her green hat with a feather in it. I let him wear my green T-shirt with his gumboots. We didn't have leggings, but Miss Heatherbell painted Dom's legs a nice green to match. He wanted to make a bow and some arrows, but I secretly told him that might frighten Wodge.

Arlo and Sammi arrived together and we went out onto the back lawn.

'So what is it?' asked Arlo. He always seemed to know when something was happening, even if he didn't know *what*.

So we told them. At least, we told them bits.

Friends always trust friends, but we didn't want them to think we'd gone crazy.

'So, there are things at the bottom of the garden,' said Arlo. 'Are they dangerous?'

'Not so far,' I said. 'But one of them does do a deadly fartish sort of thing.'

Dom was quick to say, 'We're not really sure which part of him the smell comes from.' Then he said, 'The other one tries to do magic. But she's not very good at it.'

I could see Arlo starting to look doubtful about all this. 'Show us,' he said.

Sammi's eyes were shining, in spite of the threat of a deadly fart. 'Yes! I'd love to see these things!'

We decided to risk it. But only if Arlo and Sammi waited while Dom and I went in first.

This time Wodge didn't hide when he heard us coming. He came waddling to meet us.

'Bringeth ice-cream?' he asked.

We explained that we had brought two new friends.

'They're brilliant at secrets,' I promised.

The BTF, of course, was cranky.

'Oh yes,' she whinged. 'Bring your friends. Bring the whole town. Just tell them it's a secret and we'll be fine, fine, fine!'

Arlo must have got tired of waiting. Maybe the guinea pigs showed the way again. All I know is that Arlo and Sammi came crawling through after us. With the BTF shouting the way she was, nobody heard them coming until they were in.

'Begoned!' yelped Wodge. 'Spy-peoples cometh!' And he tumbled into his hole.

'Pooh!' Arlo reeled backwards. Sammi pulled the edge of her headscarf across her nose.

'Breathe through your mouth,' I croaked. 'It won't last long.'

The BTF said nothing. She was just a piece of stone again.

Then Sammi did something strange. 'The poor thing is frightened,' she said.

She walked over to where Wodge was hiding under the gargoyle. It was as if, to her, the Wodge-pong had floated away. Sammi sat down and began to sing. The song didn't seem to have words, just a calm and gentle tune that Sammi crooned and hummed.

After a few moments, the gargoyle began to tip back. Wodge slowly climbed out of his hole and sat beside Sammi. He gazed at her as though she was working some kind of enchantment. Sammi began to stroke him as she came to the end of her song.

We were all very quiet. Then it was the BTF who spoke. For once, she didn't sound bad-tempered.

'I know that. It's an old, old song. A Do Not Be Afraid song. Nobody knows where it came from — just like Wodge.'

By that time, Arlo was ready to believe anything. Or maybe he was a little bit dazed by the song. But a talking statue didn't flabbergast him as much as it might have done. It certainly didn't flabbergast Sammi.

'How do you know that song, Sammi?' I asked.

'My mother sings it,' she said simply.

CHAPTER FOURTEEN

Whatever the mystery of the song, Wodge was won over. He smiled at all of us.

'Ice-cream?' he asked hopefully, as if we might have a dollop or two in our pockets.

'Is ice-cream all you ever eat?' I asked him. 'What else can you eat around here?'

The BTF gave a haughty sniff. 'Oh, he manages just fine. A little nibble of grass, a chew on some leaves, a sip of rainwater. And he does have other ways to get what he likes.'

Wodge closed his eyes, screwed up his nose and waggled his ears.

'He's thinking,' said the BTF. 'It can take a long time.'

After a while, Wodge stopped thinking and began bouncing around. 'Wodge hath had much thought, yay!' he chortled. 'Very good friend Will Shakespeare said "There are more things in heaven and earth than ice-cream." Wodge shall show thee. We shall go friendishly to the park-place.'

That couldn't be right.

'You mean out of here?' I asked. 'I thought you were scared of being captured.'

Wodge gave a shrug. 'Not all the time is Wodge *Wodge*.'

Arlo got that straight away. 'OK,' he said. 'So who are you when you're not Wodge?'

Wodge took a deep breath. He screwed up his face and grunted so hard I thought he was going to do more than just a smell. *Humph, humph, humph.*

Then, 'Wow! How cool is that?' Arlo whistled.

Wodge's curls were now tight and woolly and black. His legs were long and skinny and he skipped around wagging a stubby little tail. 'Baaa!' he bleated.

'It's a lamb!' gasped Dom.

'Well, sort of,' said the BTF. 'If you don't look too closely. I have met better shape-shifters than him.'

Sammi was much kinder. 'The genies in our stories back home are famous for shape-shifting, and Wodge seems as good as any of them,' she said.

That pleased Wodge so much that he did a poodle, a rabbit and a knitted beanie, one after the other. Then he turned back into himself and cried, 'Parkwards we go!'

'Oh yes,' moaned the BTF. 'Off you go to the park. Have a nice time, won't you? Don't worry about me, stuck here for the last hundred years!'

'Oh dear!' I said. 'We'd like to take you with us. But you are a bit of a lump.'

That was it. 'A lump?' bawled the BTF. 'Who are you calling a lump? I'm skinnier than you are! Can I help it if I'm made of stone?'

It was Sammi who came to the rescue. 'Don't worry,' she said. 'I've got an idea.'

We all looked at her and waited.

'We've got an old pram,' she said. 'It's been in our shed since Yasmin got too big for it.'

Dom gave the BTF a pat on the head. 'You'd like to go for a ride in a pram, wouldn't you?'

The BTF didn't reply. She was probably still sulking about being called a lump.

Sammi scrambled out and went through the side gate to fetch the pram. Then Arlo asked the BTF something I'd been wondering myself.

'OK, how did you get to be here in the first place?'

The BTF still wasn't speaking, so Wodge answered for her. 'Shipwise. After her mis-happening spellwise with the fiddler, she was field-stuck for much moons. At last a farmbloke discovereth her. Then, getting it in his head to sail Australiawards, he bringeth her with him for the beautifulness of his garden. He plonketh her here near Wodge's hole and forgetteth her.'

That must have been the man who built the house we were staying in. Miss Heatherbell had told us her father had bought it ages and ages ago, and it had been built for a while even then. But that part of the garden had always stayed forgotten, even back when Miss Heatherbell had found Wodge and the BTF when she was my age. All these things I'd written in my notebook, partly for my Awesome Girl stories and also because it was part of the true story of Wodge and the BTF.

Sammi came back with the pram OK, but we still had a problem. No way could we get it through the bushes to the BTF.

'No worries,' said Arlo. 'We'll just drag her out.'

So we tipped the BTF over. Arlo and I grabbed her feet and Dom and Sammi grabbed her arms. We crawled backwards and pulled. They crawled forwards and pushed. The BTF shrieked and howled, while Wodge came muttering and bumbling

115

along at the back. But at last we made it out onto the lawn to the sound of twenty guinea pigs cheering.

CHAPTER FIFTEEN

We managed to lift the BTF into the pram, and propped her up so that she could see. Then off we went, out through the side gate and down the road to the park. We took it in turns to push, with Wodge, looking a lot like a fat puppy, toddling along beside us.

It was the first time that the BTF had been anywhere in a hundred years, and she was having the best time. She showed her happiness by grumbling.

Cars were noisy, smelly beasts. Houses were ugly and there were too many shops full of rubbishy stuff. She was loving it.

The park near us is huge. It has a big picnic and barbecue area with a play park at one end. Then, through some fancy iron gates, there's a part that's all flowers and statues and fountains.

As we got to the barbecue area, Wodge began to get excited. 'Childlings!' he burbled. 'Childlings are best!'

The BTF gave a snort. 'Now he's going to show you how he gets his food.'

We all cried out in horror at once. 'He doesn't eat *children*?'

''Course he doesn't,' cackled the BTF. 'But watch!'

Because it was Sunday, there were a lot of people and a lot of kids. There was also a lot of food.

One family had put a tray of cooked sausages

on a picnic table. The mother had gone back to the barbecue. The father was buttering bread rolls. A boy of about four was standing on the bench sniffing the sausages.

Wodge, in his cute little doggie disguise, trotted up to the boy, staying well out of sight of the parents. He gazed up with huge, longing eyes and wagged his tail. Then he sat up and begged.

The boy giggled softly. Making sure that nobody was watching, he picked up a sausage from the tray and dropped it down to Wodge. Just as secretly, Wodge caught it. Then he trotted back to us, noisily gulping down the sausage.

'Is that stealing?' asked Sammi anxiously.

'Nah,' scoffed the BTF. 'Wodge never steals. He gets food given to him.'

'But only by kids,' laughed Arlo. 'Grown-ups might not be so generous.'

In the next ten minutes, with some secret shape-shifting in the shrubbery, under benches and in other nifty hiding places, Wodge scored two more sausages, a fishcake and a lamington – all from little kids.

We pushed the pram through into the garden part of the park. I thought that Wodge might have had enough to eat, but I'd forgotten how much he loved ice-cream.

We came to a secluded and leafy spot where two mums were standing having a chat on the footpath. They both had babies in strollers. One baby was asleep. The other one, a bit bigger, was happily making a mess with an ice-cream cone.

Wodge did his *humph, humph* and became a lamb. He wasn't a real one this time, but a very woolly toy lamb. He skipped up to the stroller, and he didn't even have to beg. The chortling baby happily pushed her ice-cream into his mouth.

Slurp, slurp, gulp and the ice-cream was gone. Neither mum had noticed a thing. But Wodge had at last had enough.

'Yum, yum, belly all fullness and legs all weariness,' he mumbled. So Sammi picked him up and put him in the pram.

Arlo and I were taking our turn at pushing, when along the path came Mrs Biddlethorpe. Everybody knew Mrs Biddlethorpe. She was in charge of our school canteen. She was in charge of the tennis club. She was in charge of St Mark's choir. She was in charge of a lot of things. And Mrs Biddlethorpe liked to swoop, just like a seagull after a hot chip. Right now, she was swooping on us.

'Oh, you lovely, lovely children!' she cried. 'Taking the darling baby for a walk!' The sparkly bits on her glasses frames shone as brightly as her teeth as she peered into the pram.

Then she reeled back.

'Oh, you naughty, naughty children!' she shrieked. 'You have stolen a statue from the park! Put it back at once, or I shall have to call a park-keeper!'

I wasn't sure how we were going to get out of this – until another voice spoke.

'Ho, it's perfickerly all right, madam! Us statues like a little outing now and then. Nice of the kiddies to think of it.'

124

The voice came from a large statue of a famous explorer sitting on his horse. I forget his name.

Mrs Biddlethorpe stared, open-mouthed.

'I'd *really* like to go for a gallop!' said the horse. 'Galloping, galloping, over the fence. Galloping over the paddocks. Galloping up the hill ...'

'OK,' said the explorer. 'You can shut up about it now.'

Mrs Biddlethorpe sat down on a bench. Her face had gone the colour of a tomato and she fanned herself with her hat. Sammi went over to her.

'Don't worry, Mrs B,' she said. 'Weird things can happen sometimes, especially on a hot day. I'm sure you'll feel fine very soon.'

We weren't sure if that made it OK with Mrs Biddlethorpe.

Anyway, we decided to go home as soon as we could. Keeping away from barbecues, we went through the play park. That was a big mistake.

CHAPTER SIXTEEN

Who should be hanging about on the swings but Stewie MacGubbin and his gang. There were four of them: Stewie, Dan, Tyson and Zig. As soon as I saw them, I knew we were in trouble.

Stewie slid off his swing. 'Look who it is,' he sneered. 'Nancy Pantsy, Dummy dum-dum and their little friends. Who've you got in your pram then? Your teddy or your dolly?'

They spread out in front of us and there was no way we were going to get past them.

'Come on,' said Stewie. 'Show us.' He sniggered and his mates all sniggered after him. 'Everybody at school tomorrow is going to love knowing that you lot still like to play with a teddy.' He took a step towards us, still grinning.

There was a loud *humph, humph, humph*. Out of the pram hurtled a hairy caterpillar about the size of a cat. It wriggled furiously across to Stewie and leapt up onto his chest.

Stewie screamed. His eyes rolled and his hair stood on end, just like the caterpillar's. He flapped his hands and fell over backwards screaming, 'Get it off me! Get it off me!'

None of his mates were game to do that, and none of us really wanted to. But the caterpillar finally dropped off by itself and wriggled away. Stewie lurched to his feet and ran. The rest of his gang gaped after him. But without Stewie, they didn't know what to do.

'I wonder if everybody at school tomorrow will love knowing that Stewie MacGubbin still wets his pants,' mused Arlo.

'Better get home,' I said. 'There's going to be trouble about this, for sure. Stewie's going to want his revenge.' I called out to Wodge. 'Come on, hop in the pram. We're going.'

But there was no sign of Wodge.

'He's gone,' said Arlo. 'Run away.'

Dom and Sammi were already gazing all around the playground, but it was empty.

'The poor thing's probably frightened,' said Sammi. She sounded worried.

An angry snort came from the pram. 'Fed-up more like! Had enough!' The BTF sounded fed-up herself.

'But he will come back, won't he?' I asked.

If the BTF had been able to shrug, she would've. 'Maybe he will and maybe he won't.' Then she went on in her super-bossy voice, 'It's all your fault. If you hadn't come stickybeaking around the bottom of Miss Heatherbell's garden, you'd never have found Wodge and me. Stewie would never have poked his nose over the fence. If you had never taken us out in the pram, Stewie would never have tried to bully us. Now look what's happened!'

We'd never seen Sammi get really angry before, but she had a fierce, eye-flashing glare on her face

131

right now. 'It was *my* idea to bring the pram, and it was for you, so you didn't get left behind! How ungrateful can you be?' she scolded.

That was enough to make the BTF go into her statue mood and she wouldn't say another word.

'OK,' said Arlo. 'He's little and pudgy and he's got short legs. He can't have got very far, can he? Let's go!'

We tried so hard to find Wodge. Taking it in turns to push the BTF in the pram, we searched every centimetre of the park. We called, 'Wodge! Come back, Wodge!'

One elderly man kindly asked us who Roger was, but we couldn't explain. Nor could we ask people if they'd seen a ginormous hairy caterpillar.

Arlo said that Wodge had probably turned himself into something else by now. We carefully looked at every dog we met.

'I don't think we're going to find him,' said Dom. Even in his brave Robin Hood hat, he sounded close to tears. Sammi already was in tears. I felt especially sorry for the BTF. She was the crankiest fairy you could ever meet. Now she was going to be a cranky, lonely fairy. I asked her if she'd like to come and live in our garden after Dad got home. But she said she wanted to live where she'd always lived. 'I don't need your sympathy, thank you very much!'

I knew she wasn't feeling nearly as cranky as she sounded – she was trying to hide how miserable she felt.

So we took her back to where we'd first found her.

It was really sad to have to leave her there on her own. Dom and Sammi gave her a hug. 'The clunkiest hug I ever gave,' Dom told me later. 'People made of stone aren't very cuddly.'

'We'll come and visit you,' Sammi promised the BTF.

'Don't bother,' the little statue sniffed.

So we all went miserably home. Arlo helped
Sammi to push the pram back to her place. When
Dom and I got inside, Miss Heatherbell was
brilliantly happy with her new rainbow hair colours.
We did our best to be happy with her, but it was
hard work.

Then Dad called us on Miss Heatherbell's phone. He had forgotten to let us know he'd arrived in Antarctica, but he was telling us now. He was happy, too, and he'd met Brian the elephant seal. Dad was sure they were going to be great friends. That only reminded us that we'd found a friend in Wodge the Whatever, but we'd lost him.

I'll say one thing – Stewie MacGubbin is tough. By teatime, he'd got over his fright and was ringing Miss Heatherbell's doorbell again. Dom and I hid behind a pink unicorn and listened.

'Excuse me, Miss Heatherbell, I don't know if you have a rule about no pets, but I thought you'd like to know that Dum-dum boy and his sister who live in your house have got a man-eating caterpillar. They push it around in a pram.' Stewie even had his shark smile back.

Miss Heatherbell looked at Stewie up and down. Then she answered with her own, much sweeter smile. 'Really, dear? Isn't that nice? I must say, I'm more of a guinea pig person myself.'

CHAPTER SEVENTEEN

After tea I went up to my room and tried to start writing a story, just to give my brain something new to think about. But my brain went *duh, err, blah, clunk* and then switched itself back to what-ifs.

What if Wodge had come home after all? What if he was sitting down there waiting to demand ice-cream?

What if I just nicked down to see?

There was still about half an hour of daylight, so

I went quietly downstairs and out the back door.

The first thing I saw was Dom in his Merlin cloak plodding towards the house. He didn't look like somebody bringing good news.

'Nope,' he sighed. 'Just her. And she told me that if I didn't rack off, she'd turn me into a guinea pig and nobody'd know which one was me.'

My heart sank like one of Dad's home-made sponge cakes, but I felt even sorrier for Dom.

'Don't you worry,' I told him. 'She doesn't know how to do that. If she did, both you and I would be guinea pigs by now.'

139

'What about Wodge?' asked Dom.

'Nah,' I said. 'I reckon in her own ratty way she's fond of Wodge. She wouldn't turn him into a guinea pig.'

Then I realised, not for the first time, that my little brother is one smart kid.

'But what if Wodge turned *himself* into a guinea pig?' said Dom. 'He could be running around laughing at us because we can't spot him right under our noses.'

As if to show how likely that was, a whole bunch of guinea pigs came scuttling across the lawn towards us. Black with white splodges, brown with ginger splodges – every kind of guinea pig, plain or splodged, was now woofling around our feet.

I still didn't have much idea of who was who, but Dom had learnt most of their names – Ron, Polly, Norman, Gloria, Wilfred and … Wodge!

There he was, a dear little toffee-coloured guinea

pig with extra big and shiny eyes, who unfortunately took off like a cheetah in a hurry the minute Dom called his name. But yay! He was running home! What a relief to see that furry little bottom disappear into the grass between the shed and the greenhouse.

'Let's go and tell him how sorry we are,' I said. 'And maybe he'll get over it.'

By the time we'd wriggled through to the BTF's spot, Wodge was already happily hopping and nose-twitching around her toes.

'See, Wodge is home!' I sang. 'You have to be happy about that.'

'This is Violet,' grated the BTF. 'She has always been Violet.'

Oh.

'She seems quite a bit like Wodge,' said Dom hopefully. 'Are you sure she's not him?'

But Violet was already heading back to her pack.

'OK,' snapped the BTF. 'Here's something you two need to get into your thick heads. Wodge can change his shape, but he can't change his size. He can be a lamb, a dog, a cat. He can be a wombat-sized flea. But he can't be an ant-sized ant, or an elephant-sized elephant. And he can't be a guinea pig-sized guinea pig. It just doesn't work.'

Well, that made looking for him a whole lot easier. Any ants or elephants we came across wouldn't be him.

Dom was already working on another plan, one that I quickly caught on to.

'What's Wodge's favourite ice-cream in the whole world?' he asked.

'Ah well,' said the BTF. 'That would have to be the one he had in China about two-and-a-half thousand years ago. King Tang of Shang had ninety-four men make a mountain of the stuff for Wodge to waffle through.'

I took out my notebook, ready to write down the recipe.

'Buffalo milk, flour and … there was a secret ingredient.' She seemed to be thinking hard. 'Hang on, Wodge did tell me …'

Please, I silently begged. *Remember the secret ingredient.*

'Broccoli! It was broccoli!'

'Blech!' said Dom, who wasn't a big fan of broccoli. I had to agree, it was a peculiar ice-cream flavour. But then, Wodge was a peculiar kind of whatever he was. And then there was the buffalo milk.

'Why couldn't he have liked choc-chip best?' I sighed.

The BTF was revving up to full cranky-pants again. 'What does it matter? He's halfway back to China now and it's *all your fault!*'

'Come on, Dom,' I said miserably. 'Time to go.'

Much later, when Dom and I were supposed to be in bed, we leant out of our bedroom windows.

It was a warm, still night and a bright pink owl soared over our heads. But nothing could make us feel good.

'The BTF is right,' said Dom. 'It *is* all our fault. Wodge trusted us to keep him a secret and we messed up. I bet Dad wouldn't let Stewie frighten Brian.'

I wasn't sure that an elephant seal would be too worried about Stewie. But Dom was right. Wodge was our friend, and we'd let him down big time.

CHAPTER EIGHTEEN

'Buffalo milk?'

It was Monday morning and the four of us were at Arlo's place, sitting in the backyard.

'Where are we going to get buffalo milk?' asked Arlo again.

Dom had told us his plan, and it was so simple it might work. The plan was to get a big cardboard box and take it to the park. Put a tub of Wodge's favourite ice-cream inside. Then just hide and wait. If Wodge was still around, even if he were blindfolded and had marshmallows stuffed in his ears and a bucket on his head, he'd find that ice-cream. So all we'd have to do was jump out and close the box. Easy.

But first we had to find some buffalo milk. Or at least find a buffalo and milk it.

'I bet Superman could milk a buffalo,' said Dom, who just happened to be that superhero today.

'My mum's working at the Whole World Café today,' said Sammi. 'I don't think they have buffalo milk, but they do have sheep's milk. And they definitely have an ice-cream machine.'

'There's a difference between a sheep and a buffalo,' I said, but Dom didn't think that was a problem.

'Wodge probably won't notice,' he said, 'if we put in plenty of flour and broccoli.'

'Right,' said Arlo, 'we're onto it.'

We collected a cool bag from his mum's kitchen
and a big box from the gallery storeroom. Then
we went and fetched the pram from Sammi's place.
The little kids were in creche, so there was nobody
at home, but the pram was where it always was.

We put the box on the pram and pushed it to the
Whole World Café.

Mrs Yusef was pleased to see us, but we had to
wait a while until she was free to serve us.

'You want what?' she asked when we ordered,
probably thinking she hadn't heard quite correctly.

'A tub of ice-cream, please,' I repeated. 'Sheep's
milk, flour and broccoli, to take away.'

'It's OK, Mum,' said Sammi, 'Arlo's got his
pocket money.'

I don't think payment was what her mother was wondering about, but the café had sheep's milk, flour and broccoli, so she shrugged and got on with it. Maybe she thought this was an Australian treat she hadn't discovered before.

It was going to take twenty minutes to make the ice-cream, and Sammi said we should go and get the BTF.

'Do we have to?' I groaned. 'Whinge, whinge, snivel, gripe and grizzle.'

'She's lost her friend,' said Sammi. 'We mustn't leave her all alone.'

So we sneaked back and got the BTF and put her in the pram. She complained bitterly about the cardboard box on top of her, but we weren't going to carry it.

Back at the Whole World Café, Sammi and Dom sat in the garden area and looked after the pram while Arlo and I went in to get the ice-cream.

Mrs Yuself gave us a motherly smile. 'I put some semolina in,' she said. 'Just to make it a little nicer.'

OK, now to find out how good Dom's plan was.

As we pushed the pram along the street, we kept our eyes open for anything that might be Wodge. We saw plenty of birds, blowies, and even a cocky that screeched 'bog off!' at us from somebody's veranda.

I thought the BTF would screech back, but she'd gone all stony about the box.

We were halfway down Laurel Avenue when we spotted him crouched in the bottom of a hedge.

He was big and blue and fluffy and he looked like a rabbit. Of course. We'd forgotten that Wodge did stuffed animals as well as live ones. But that wouldn't stop him pouncing on the ice-cream. Dom took the ice-cream out of the cool bag and we set up the trap, with our fingers crossed that Wodge wouldn't twig as to what the box was for.

Wodge didn't move.

'Ice-cream!' Dom showed him the tub, but Wodge totally ignored it. That was not like him.

'He's still upset with us,' said Sammi sadly.

Arlo lifted Wodge out of the hedge and pushed the ice-cream under his fluffy, blue nose. 'Come on, mate, your favourite!'

But Wodge was still playing hard to please.

'What do you think you're doing?'

None of us had seen the woman coming. She had a person of about three holding her hand and glowering at us.

'Why are you pushing Flipflop's nose into that ice-cream?' demanded the mother.

'Mine!' screamed the child, reaching out for Wodge.

The woman snatched the rabbit from Arlo's hands and gave it to her little boy.

'There you are, Elton, and please don't lose him again.'

Elton grabbed the rabbit upside-down by one leg, which Wodge would never have stood for. So we just watched them march away.

'I could have told you that wasn't Wodge,' growled a voice from the pram.

'So why didn't you?' I retorted.

Arlo shoved the ice-cream into the cool bag while I plonked the cardboard box back on top of the BTF. This search was not going to be easy.

CHAPTER NINETEEN

'Dom, I'm not sure it's going to work.' Arlo said what we were all thinking. Wodge was keeping well out of sight. Worse still, he could be hundreds of kilometres away by now and would never live at the bottom of Miss Heatherbell's garden again.

It was a miserable thought, and even Dom's Superman cape couldn't make him look the least bit super. We were wheeling the pram past Mrs Biddlethorpe's house when we saw a fat Persian cat with a face as sour as the BTF's glaring down at us from the garden wall. It was Wodge-sized, sure enough, but we'd learnt our lesson. Whoever it was, it would have to pass the sheep's milk, broccoli and semolina ice-cream test.

The cat watched with a sneer as we set up the trap, and my hopes were not high. But the second the lid came off the ice-cream, the scowling face became seriously alert and the cat jumped down off the wall.

After that, it was too easy. Nobody in the world but Wodge could have guzzled and slurped that gross ice-cream with such gusto. I whipped the tub away before he finished the lot and Arlo gave him a hefty nudge into the box and closed the flaps.

'Gotcha!' crowed Dom.

Wodge obviously didn't like being in the box, and there was a heap of yowling and scrabbling as we lifted it onto the pram. The BTF was still saying nothing.

Fortunately, it wasn't far to Miss Heatherbell's house, and we successfully got in through the side gate. But what we had forgotten to work out was how to get the box through the bushes. And that couldn't be done.

'We're going to have to open the box and gently coax him out,' said Sammi. 'Once he sees where he is, he'll be happy.'

The opening of the box happened OK, but the

gentle coaxing didn't. Wodge hurtled out with bared teeth and lashing claws, glaring furiously. Before we could grab him, which wasn't a good idea anyway, he was over the fence and away. We'd lost him again.

'Wodge doesn't want come home, does he?'
Sammi sounded tearful.

A scornful voice came from the pram. 'That
wasn't Wodge. Nothing like him. Just a greedy guts
moggy that'll eat anything.'

Before we could say or do anything else, Mrs
Pikelet appeared at the back door.

'Lunch!' she called.

'Stay there!' I warned the BTF.

'What else can I do?' she howled as we trooped
inside.

We were halfway through a pile of salad
sandwiches when Miss Heatherbell rolled into the
kitchen with her phone in her lap.

'Something lovely and helpful for you to do,
darlings,' she said. 'Mrs MacWotsit from next door
just rang. The one with the tittly-tattly son. She's
letting all the neighbours know that her friend Mrs
Biddlethorpe has lost her cat. It seems Mrs B was

having a meeting of her poetry group and she's terribly upset because while they were busy making up poems, her cat disappeared. It could be that somebody stole him.'

All four of us looked at each other.

'Her cat?' asked Dom in a small voice.

'His name is Charles, apparently,' replied Miss Heatherbell. 'He's a grey Persian and he never goes anywhere. But today he did. Poof! Vanished into thin air.' She smiled warmly. 'But I told Mrs MacGoobly you'd be happy to help look for Charles.'

Happy or not, we had to look for Charles. We had to find him and give him back to Mrs Biddlethorpe. But perhaps without mentioning that it was us who had stolen him.

Ten minutes later we set off again with the pram, the box, and what was left of the ice-cream.

Of course, there was no sign of Charles in the lane. When we last saw him, he didn't look as if he was going to hang about.

'Perhaps he's found his own way home,' said Dom hopefully.

'Let's go and see,' I said. But the way things

163

were turning out today, Charles returning home by himself would be much too easy.

CHAPTER TWENTY

When we arrived at Mrs Biddlethorpe's gate, it was obvious that Charles had not come home. Mrs Biddlethorpe and her poetry group were still searching. We hadn't come across a search party anywhere else, so perhaps not many neighbours were upset about Charles's disappearance.

But in Mrs Biddlethorpe's garden, poets were crawling under bushes, banging on the drainpipes and even upending the garbage bin, all the time calling out:

'Cat, dear cat, where did you roam?

Oh, pussy dear,

Won't you please come home?'

And:

'Charlie, Barley, whatever your name,

You're getting too old for this silly game.'

Mrs Biddlethorpe was calling:

'Charles, my dearest, come back to me

And you shall have kippers and cream for tea.'

Well, they were a poetry group.

So, we still had a chance of finding Charles and returning him to where he belonged.

Mrs Biddlethorpe did, of course, have one other good friend she had called – not a poet, but Mrs MacGubbin, mother of Stewie. And now he and his

gang came down the street, not looking so much for Charles as for trouble. The last thing we needed was for them to catch us with the pram again.

'Quick!' We tore round the corner and down Ripley Road, with me pushing the pram, Arlo and Sammi holding the box steady and Dom carrying the cool bag with the ice-cream. Dom was the only one able to look backwards.

'It's all right,' he panted at last. 'They're not coming.'

We stopped to get our breath back and to check on the BTF.

'OK?' I asked her.

'Of course,' she snarled. 'If there's one thing I love, it's going ninety kilometres an hour in a bumpy old pram with a box on top of me.'

'Listen!' whispered Dom. He sounded so excited that we all went quiet.

Meow. It was coming from behind a garbage bin that somebody hadn't taken in.

Meow.

'We're going to have to be very careful about this,' I said.

Luckily, there was enough ice-cream left to bait the trap one more time. We moved the pram so that we could crouch behind it to watch and wait.

We didn't have to wait long. Charles's grey, grumpy face slid around from the back of the bin and the rest of him followed. You wouldn't have thought he'd fall for the same trick twice, but he did. Slurp, slurp, guzzle, a gentle shove and we'd done it again. We left the ice-cream in the box with Charles this time, and it made for a much quieter trip back to Mrs Biddlethorpe's house.

We were just pushing the pram up to her gate, feeling pretty pleased with ourselves, when we discovered we'd been ambushed yet again. There was the sound of running feet and Stewie MacGubbin wrenched the pram handle from my hands. Tyson and Zig grabbed the box and they rushed the whole thing through the gate. We could only follow and hope for the best.

'Mrs Biddlethorpe, these kids kidnapped your little pussycat! But we rescued him!' Stewie was more than usually vomit-inducing. The flaps of the box were opened and Charles stalked out.

'Oh, my precious!' Mrs Biddlethorpe scooped him up in her arms. Well, I thought, Wodge is gone

forever, but at least Charles is home.

But then ... POOH!

Mrs Biddlethorpe reeled backwards and the cat leapt free and streaked away. Urk!! The poets staggered around with hands and hankies over their noses. Mrs Biddlethorpe moaned and flapped the air, the MacGubbin gang ran away gagging and Stewie was sick into the lupins. Arlo, Sammi, Dom and I remembered to breathe through our mouths and managed to escape most of the pong.

Then a poet with a moustache and ponytail pointed to the roof of Mrs Biddlethorpe's porch and croaked. Those of us who were able to, looked to where he was pointing. A fat, grey Persian cat was crouched on the roof, gazing down with a snooty sneer. Then, in a voice that went with his face, he drawled:

'For goodness sake, stop your squealing and squawking,

And listen to me while I'm talking.

The pong, I agree, is rather strong,

But if you think it was me who made it, you're wrong!'

That caused a lot of jaws to drop and eyes to pop, and everything went very quiet. Then the BTF

cackled gleefully at her own cleverness. She'd used her ventriloquism to tell us that the cat on the porch roof wasn't Wodge and, as a bonus, had stunned all the poets just for fun. If that pong hadn't come from the cat, it meant Wodge was still in the neighbourhood. We decided to grab the pram and go.

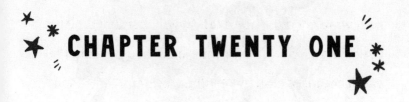

CHAPTER TWENTY ONE

It was time to get back to the Wodge hunt. But where to start? My head was whirling and I needed to think.

'Can we sit down?' I asked, as we came to a bench.

So the four of us sat, with the BTF in the pram beside us, and I took out my notebook. I had heaps written in there about Wodge, the BTF and the astonishing house. I began to read through my notes to look for clues.

When I'd been writing *Awesome Girl and the Haunted House,* I'd asked Miss Heatherbell how old her house was. She said she thought it had been built around 1900. That was well over a hundred years ago. Wodge had told us that the BTF had come to Australia with the man who built the house, and he'd left her beside Wodge's hole. And she'd been there ever since.

'More than a hundred years!' I exclaimed. 'That's

a very long friendship.' Did we really think that Wodge would run away and leave the BTF for good after all that time?

'I don't think so,' said Sammi. 'Not unless he was really scared.'

But *would* he be that scared? Twice he'd chased Stewie off with his caterpillar trick, and he knew he could always do it again. I went back to my notebook. Wodge had been friends with Alexander the Great, a mighty warrior, and he'd maybe even been into battle. Would Wodge seriously be scared of a spotty-nosed fifth-grader?

Arlo didn't think so. 'I reckon he just went off feeling a bit cranky. He'd have got over it.'

I flipped through the pages. 'Last night I wrote down the recipe for his very favourite ice-cream. How did he know this afternoon to shapeshift himself into Charles and hide behind those bins so that he'd get some of that ice-cream?'

177

We all looked at each other. 'He knew!' said Dom. 'He knew about my plan. It's the only explanation. He knew we'd nabbed Charles by mistake and then lost him, so it was easy for him to disguise himself as Charles. He knew everything!'

Indignantly, I stuck my face into the pram and growled at the BTF. 'He knew because he *did* come home last night, didn't he? You fibbed to us! Wodge was hiding in the grass when you gave me that recipe. He knew we wanted it for something, and he meant to find out what.'

At least the BTF didn't deny it. She didn't go stony either. She laughed the longest, loudest witch-like cackle I'd ever heard, even from her. I held my breath, because a girl was jogging past and it wasn't the kind of laugh that usually comes out of a baby's pram. But luckily the girl had her earphones plugged into her phone and didn't even glance at us.

'We had the biggest laugh, me and Wodge!' The BTF was actually sounding cheerful.

I nodded. 'I bet you did! Wodge has followed us all day, hasn't he? And we were kind enough to bring you along, just so you could enjoy the joke!'

So Wodge had been in Arlo's backyard when we worked out the plan. We should have known we wouldn't see him, even when we looked. Wodge was brilliant at not being seen. He could sneak and

179

hide like nobody else because he'd been doing it for years and years. That was in my notebook too: *He doesn't want to be famous, bubble brain! He doesn't want to be on the telly.* That was what the BTF had told us when we first discovered them, back when Wodge had kept diving into his hole to hide.

'All right,' I said firmly to the BTF, whose cackles had shrunk to chuckles. 'So where has he gone now?'

'How would I know?' she answered. 'He just stank at that Biddlethorpe woman and ran. Could be anywhere.'

Did it matter? No doubt Wodge would come back home tonight again anyway. But Dom wasn't having that.

'So Wodge has proven he's a real smartypants, but what if we track him down? That'd teach him that we can be just as smart.'

I sighed. 'I like the idea, Dom. But I've run out

of notes, so there are no more clues.'

'Ah well,' said Arlo. 'That notebook of yours has been handy. But it can't tell us everything.'

Sammi gave a sigh even bigger than mine. 'He could be anywhere in the whole world.'

Ping! Yes! Of course!

'The Whole World Café!' I cried. 'He followed us there this morning and heard us order his favourite ice-cream. He had plenty of time to look around before we took off again. And what do you think he saw at the Whole World Café?'

'Food,' said Arlo. 'Fabulous food. Especially ice-cream.'

'A garden with tables and chairs and swings,' said Sammi.

'And kids,' shouted Dom.

'Wodge heaven,' I sang out, 'let's go!'

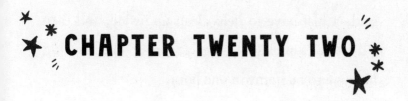

CHAPTER TWENTY TWO

By the time we got to the Whole World Café, it was almost ready to close. There was just one customer inside, and the waiter had begun wiping down the tables. We parked the BTF and the pram and went round the back. Mrs Yusef had just loaded a tray with crockery and was on her way inside. As always, she was delighted to see us.

'Hello!' she smiled. 'I hope you enjoyed your special ice-cream.'

'It was enjoyed,' I promised her.

Mrs Yusef looked at her watch. 'Samira,' she said. 'I just have to help clean up inside, and then I'll fetch Yasmin and Jameela from creche. I would like you to be home in one hour.'

'OK, Mum.' Sammi and Dom made a beeline for the swings, which was a perfect excuse for us being there. Then Mrs Yusef said, 'There was a pussy cat out here this afternoon. He was very big and beautiful, and very, very hungry. The children gave him ice-cream and that made him purr.'

I bet it did!

'I don't know where he belongs, poor creature,' Mrs Yusef went on. 'I've never seen him here before. But I don't think he had eaten for a long time.'

'We'll look for him!' offered Arlo, just as I was about to.

So Mrs Yusef went inside, and we got to work searching. It didn't take as long as we'd thought.

Dom heard it first. 'What's that humming?' he asked. 'Like a bee?'

'No,' said Sammi. 'Whining, like a mosquito.'

'It's both,' I said. 'It's snoring.'

Sure enough, there he was, curled up fast asleep at the back of a hydrangea bush. The cat disguise had long worn off, and it was an unmistakable Wodge who rolled over and opened one bleary eye.

'Don't you dare stink us!' said Arlo.

But Wodge only mumbled, 'Belly all fullness and Wodge all sleepiness.' Then he let out one of his well-known burps.

So we carried him to the pram and tucked him in beside the BTF.

'OK,' I said sternly. 'Time to go home. And I mean home!'

Later that night, when Dom and I were supposed to be in bed, we leant out of our bedroom windows. A familiar bright-pink owl was gliding over the backyard.

We listened carefully and could just make out the sound of two voices down at the bottom of the garden, one high-pitched and nattering, the other slow and gurgling. We had brought our friends safely home.

'They were really sneaky, weren't they?' said Dom. 'Thinking they were so clever!'

'Yes, they were,' I said.

'But we were just as clever,' said Dom. 'And we found him.'

'Yes, we did,' I said.

'Are they still our friends?' he asked.

'Yes. They are,' I said. And we looked at each other and grinned.

Under my pillow, I kept a torch for reading and writing at night. I got into bed and took out my notebook and pencil.

We were going to have to ask Miss Heatherbell to buy a lot more ice-cream in future. But that

forgetting spell *was* leaky, and there was a good chance she might vaguely remember why.

Mysteries, secrets, muddles and half-forgotten spells. My notebook was almost full. But I would start on another. This summer, I was going to write at least two Awesome Girl stories. And not now, but maybe one day, I would write the true story of Wodge, the BTF and me.